Tango with God

Aelita Ingram

ISBN: 978-1-7360310-3-2

To A.B.S. with eternal love and respect

CONTENTS

Before the closed door,
Creatures meet their fate,
Silence tells their end.

- ABAL KIN

1. TUESDAY

Beep-beep-beep… The shrill sound of the alarm clock sliced mercilessly through the hazy tranquility of the early morning, rudely awakening Laura from her restful slumber. She groaned in frustration, her face contorted in annoyance as she blindly fumbled for the elusive snooze button, struggling to bring her groggy mind into focus and shake off the stubborn remnants of sleep. The cool, crisp sheets tangled around her legs, offering a contrasting comfort against the disruptive noise that had invaded her peaceful dreams.

As she lay in bed, her eyes fixed on the textured ceiling, Laura suddenly remembered that she didn't have to go to work today. The Sunshine Coffee Shop, a cozy and charming establishment on the bustling corner of 36th Street and Como, where she had been a barista for the past year, had tragically gone bankrupt. The news still weighed heavily on her heart like a leaden anchor. Joshua Binder, the kind and elderly owner who treated his employees like cherished family members, had been forced to close the shop, leaving Laura and her close-knit colleagues jobless. The quaint shop, with its eclectic, mismatched furniture and walls adorned with vibrant local art, had been her sanctuary from the stresses of everyday life.

The thought of her former coworkers unceremoniously dismissed without pay by the new and indifferent owner left a sinking feeling in Laura's stomach. She knew that the sudden loss of income would undoubtedly upend their lives and disrupt the tight-knit community they had lovingly formed at the coffee shop. With each passing day, the harsh reality of the situation settled in, leaving Laura feeling adrift and uncertain about her future. Finding another job in the current economic climate, characterized by its unpredictability and instability, would be a formidable challenge. The coffee shop had been more than just a job – it had been a second home and a rich source of inspiration.

Laura sighed heavily as she reluctantly got out of bed, her heart heavy as she started her morning routine. She brushed a stray strand of dark hair from her face and gazed at the bright azure sky through her window. The golden sun streamed in, bathing her face in comforting warmth, while the cheerful sounds of chirping birds and the distant hum of traffic filled the air. The aroma of freshly brewed coffee, prepared by one of the neighbors, wafted in from the open window, filling the air with an enticing fragrance, a bittersweet reminder of the days she would be preparing for a busy and lively shift at the coffee shop. On those bustling mornings, the tantalizing aroma of freshly ground coffee beans and warm, flaky pastries would greet her as she stepped through the door, an olfactory embrace that promised a day of camaraderie and productivity.

Determined to shake off her melancholy, she texted her close friend Susan Donnay, an Argentine tango instructor who had always been a beacon of inspiration and unwavering support. Laura and Susan had been inseparable friends since high school, and even though they embarked on different career paths, they still stayed in touch, confiding in each other during life's challenging moments. Their friendship had weathered countless storms, and Laura knew with certainty that Susan would be there for her in this time of need.

"Hey Susan, it's Laura. How about we go to a milonga together? It's been far too long since we caught up. Let me know if you're free!"

As she typed the message, a flood of memories from their past adventures filled Laura's mind, each a treasured gem in the story of their friendship. She recalled how Susan had become utterly enamored with tango after visiting the captivating city of Buenos Aires several years ago. Since that transformative trip, Susan would eagerly travel to Argentina every year, spending weeks and sometimes months attending the enchanting milongas and taking immersive tango classes from local maestros. Through Susan's passion, Laura had discovered the vibrant and mesmerizing world of tango, and she was eternally grateful for that priceless gift.

Laura hit send, hoping that the magic of dancing would lift both their spirits and provide a temporary escape from the harsh reality they faced. As she waited for a response, Laura finished her breakfast, savoring each bite as if it were a small piece of normalcy amid the chaos. She then busied herself with getting ready for the day ahead, her mind racing with thoughts of the unknown future. She knew that life was full of unexpected twists and turns, and the only thing she could do was to adapt and make the most of whatever came her way.

2.
SUSAN

Susan's text message arrived promptly, and Laura's phone buzzed with excitement, vibrating like a tangible manifestation of her eagerness. She read the message, a radiant smile spreading across her face, filling her with anticipation.

"Hey, girl! I'm so glad you reached out. Love to go to a milonga with you. Amazing new tango dancers in town that I think you should meet. Meet me at La Catedral tonight at 9?"

To Laura the idea of meeting new dancers, each bringing their unique style and energy, was an enticing prospect.

"Sounds great, Susan! I'll be there. Can't wait to catch up and dance with some new people. Thanks for the invite!" Laura replied, her fingers dancing across the screen as she typed.

As she hit send, Laura couldn't help but reflect on how much dancing had always meant to her. From a young age, she loved to move her body to the beat of the music, the rhythm, and the melody. Dancing had always provided her with emotional and mental release from daily stresses.

Later that day, Laura dedicated herself to practicing her tango moves, transforming her living room into a makeshift dance studio. She pushed the furniture aside, creating ample space to glide and pivot, and hung a full-length mirror on one wall to observe her movements more closely. She wanted to perfect her technique, from the subtle nuances of her posture to the confident strides of her steps.

As she began her practice session, Laura focused on the fundamental elements of tango. She concentrated on her alignment, ensuring her spine was straight and her shoulders relaxed while keeping her head high. She practiced walking backward and forward, paying close attention to the smooth transfer of her weight from one foot to the other, feeling the connection between the floor and the balls of her feet.

Laura then moved on to more complex figures, such as ochos, giros, and the sensual leg movements known as "adornos." As she danced, she imagined the warm embrace of a partner, leading and following in perfect harmony. She felt the music pulsating through her body, guiding her movements as she gracefully transitioned from one step to another. Enjoying the dance, Laura felt a sense of freedom and joy, her worries momentarily dissipating into the background.

After her practice session, Laura decided to reward herself with a relaxing bath. She filled the tub with steaming water, adding a generous amount of Epsom salt to soothe her tired muscles. Finally, she lit a few scented candles around the bathroom, their flickering flames casting a soft, warm glow that enveloped the room in an intimate, serene atmosphere.

She sank into the tub, allowing the hot water to envelop her body, the tension in her muscles gradually melting. She closed her eyes and focused on the gentle sound of the water lapping against the sides of the bathtub, her thoughts drifting like the wisps of steam that rose from the water's surface. She savored this quiet moment of introspection and self-care, feeling her energy and spirit replenished.

Once she was finished with her bath, Laura wrapped herself in a plush towel and went to her bedroom to select her outfit for the evening. She opened her closet, carefully considering her options. She wanted to choose an outfit that made her feel confident and elegant and allowed for freedom of movement on the dance floor.

After much contemplation, she settled on a simple yet stunning red dress that featured a soft, flowing fabric that swirled around her legs as she moved. The dress had a flattering sweetheart neckline, accentuating her collarbones and drawing the eye to her graceful neck. To complete the look, Laura chose a pair of strappy red heels that provided support and stability while still looking chic and sophisticated. For her jewelry, she opted for a delicate silver necklace with a small tango dancer pendant, a gift from Susan that held sentimental value, and a pair of matching silver earrings that added a touch of elegance to her ensemble.

With her chosen outfit, Laura felt renewed anticipation for the evening ahead, eager to reconnect with Susan and immerse herself in the vibrant world of tango.

As the time approached to leave for the milonga, Laura felt excitement and nervous energy. She knew the evening would be filled with the comforting familiarity of Susan's presence, the thrill of meeting new dancers, and the possibility of forming new connections. She hoped that this experience would help her regain a sense of balance in her life and give her the strength to face the challenges that lay ahead.

Before leaving, Laura took a moment to center herself, standing in front of the mirror and taking a few deep, calming breaths. She looked into her own eyes and whispered words of encouragement, reminding herself that she was strong, capable, and resilient. Then, with her heart filled with hope and determination, Laura stepped out the door into the night, eager to embrace the adventures and experiences that awaited her at the milonga.

3.
MRS. FIELDING

As Laura stepped out of her apartment building and onto the street, she was greeted by the warm rays of the setting sun, casting a golden glow across the neighborhood. The air was filled with the sweet scent of blooming flowers, and she could hear the distant sound of children laughing and playing with a scrappy little dog on the sidewalk. A gentle breeze carried the chirping of birds perched on the branches of the trees lining the street, adding to the picturesque scene. It was a perfect evening, and Laura couldn't help but feel grateful for such a beautiful day.

She was just about to leave the building's premises when a familiar voice called out to her.

"Laurita! Is that you, dear?"

Laura turned to see her neighbor, Mrs. Sheila Fielding, slowly approaching her. Mrs. Fielding was in her late sixties, with curly silver hair and dull, yellowish eyes that always seemed to twinkle with curiosity. The widow of a colonel who had passed away several years ago at the

Veteran's Hospital, she had lived in the building for decades and had seen many of its residents come and go.

Colonel Fielding, her late husband, had been a pretty colorful character. He was a decorated war hero with an impressive military career, but his personal life was scandalous. Despite his marriage to Sheila, he was well-known for his many dalliances with other women. But, as a man of charm and charisma, he had a knack for making the ladies swoon, and his extramarital affairs were the talk of the town.

Sheila had somehow managed to turn a blind eye to her husband's infidelities, choosing to focus on his military accomplishments and the social status his position brought them. However, since his passing, she had become increasingly reclusive, rarely venturing outside the apartment building. Some speculated that the memories of her husband's indiscretions had finally caught up with her, while others believed she missed the excitement of being the wife of a prominent figure.

"Hello, Mrs. Fielding," Laura said with a forced smile. "How are you doing tonight?"

"Oh, I'm just fine, dear," Mrs. Fielding replied, her voice a low, almost sinister whisper. "Off to the dancing party, are we?"

Laura couldn't help but feel a wave of unease wash over her as she noticed Mrs. Fielding's intense gaze fixed on her. There was always something unsettling about her. Mrs. Fielding was known for being nosy, always curious about her neighbors and their lives. She would often sit by her window, watching the comings and goings of the residents in the building, keeping a mental log of everyone's routines.

"Yes, I'm meeting some friends there," Laura said, hoping to end the conversation quickly. "It should be a fun night."

"Ah, yes, the tango," Mrs. Fielding said with a wistful sigh. "I remember when I was young, I loved to dance. But that was a long time ago, I'm afraid."

Laura smiled politely, sensing that Mrs. Fielding was eager to engage in a conversation, likely hoping to glean some new information about her life. However, she needed to get going if she was going to make it to the milonga on time.

"Well, it was nice to see you, Mrs. Fielding," she said, edging towards the sidewalk. "But I'm afraid I have to run. I don't want to be late for the dance."

"Of course, dear, of course," Mrs. Fielding said, waving a hand. "You go ahead and have a good time."

As Laura turned the corner and disappeared, Mrs. Fielding stood on the sidewalk, watching her leave with a keen interest. Laura could still hear the distant sound of Mrs. Fielding's coughing, which echoed down the street as she walked further away.

Laura couldn't help but feel a little uneasy, knowing that Mrs. Fielding would undoubtedly be keeping a watchful eye on her. However, she tried to shake off the feeling as she continued down the street, focusing instead on the night's excitement ahead.

As she walked, Laura thought about the colonel and his reputation. It was difficult for her to imagine how Mrs. Fielding had managed to live with such a man for so long. Perhaps she had loved him deeply, or maybe she enjoyed the notoriety that came with being his wife. Either way, it was clear that his passing had left a void in her life, one she seemed to try and fill with her incessant need for gossip and information about her neighbors.

Laura pondered how Mrs. Fielding's life might have been different if she had found an outlet for her passions, as Laura had with tango. She could have been a painter, writer, or dancer herself. But now, it seemed that her only purpose was to be a passive observer of the lives of others, always curious but never quite satisfied.

4. MILONGA

Laura approached La Catedral with a sense of excitement and anticipation. The historic building, which had once been a warehouse, now stood as a monument to tango culture in the city. Its exterior had been lovingly restored, with ivy creeping up the red brick walls and ornate ironwork adorning the entrance. The vibrant atmosphere inside was palpable even from the street, as tango music spilled out through the open windows.

The warm, dimly lit interior greeted Laura as she pushed open the heavy wooden door. The room was filled with people of all ages and backgrounds coming together to share their love for tango. The high, vaulted ceiling was adorned with hanging chandeliers, casting a soft glow over the space, while the exposed brick walls were lined with art, photographs, and vintage tango memorabilia.

The dance floor itself was a work of art, crafted from polished wood and bordered by a low wall that separated it from the seating area. Surrounding the dance floor were tables covered in white tablecloths, where dancers could take a break and enjoy a glass of wine or a bite to eat. The air was filled with laughter, conversation, and the unmistakable rhythm of tango music.

As Laura made her way through the crowd, she marveled at the diverse range of people who had gathered for the milonga. From seasoned professionals in their elegant gowns and suits to enthusiastic beginners in more casual attire, the room was a melting pot of tango lovers, each bringing their unique energy and style to the dance floor.

Laura found an empty chair at a table near the edge of the dance floor and took a moment to soak in the atmosphere. She watched as couples swept across the floor, their bodies moving harmoniously with the music. The passion and intensity of their movements were mesmerizing, and Laura felt her heart swell with the desire to join them.

Her thoughts were interrupted by Susan's voice calling out to her from across the room. Her friend looked stunning in a deep red tango dress, its flowing skirt accentuating her every movement. Laura waved back, and Susan made her way over with a broad smile.

"Laura, I'm so glad you could make it!" Susan said, embracing her friend. "You look gorgeous! Are you ready to dance?"

"Absolutely," Laura replied, grinning mischievously. "Did you hear about Richie and his secret love affair with Marta from the other milonga?"

Susan gasped in surprise. "No way! I heard he was still seeing his ex-girlfriend."

Laura shook her head. "Nope, they broke up ages ago. I heard it from Gene, who heard it from Marta's sister."

The two women giggled, enjoying the juicy details of their fellow dancers' private lives. They continued to exchange rumors, each story more scandalous than the last.

Laura felt a sense of exhilaration as she reveled in the gossip and intrigue of the milonga. It was like being part of a secret club, where only the most exciting and scandalous stories were shared. She knew it was wrong to enjoy gossiping about others, but she couldn't help feeling excited about the secrets she was learning.

Over the course of the evening, Laura danced with a variety of partners, each one offering a different experience on the dance floor. Some were playful and flirtatious, while others were focused and intense, but all shared a contagious passion for the tango.

At one point, Laura's eyes landed on a man sitting alone at the bar, nursing a drink. He had a confident air about him, and Laura decided to take a chance and ask him to dance. As they began to dance, Laura realized that the man had no idea what he was doing. His movements were clumsy and awkward, and he kept stepping on her toes. Laura tried to lead him, but he seemed determined to show off his moves, no matter how misguided they were. The dance felt like a never-ending struggle, with Laura trying to salvage the situation and the man completely unaware of his incompetence. Finally, the song ended, and Laura was relieved to step away from her partner, who seemed utterly oblivious to his lack of skill.

Between dances, Laura and Susan chatted with their fellow dancers, sharing stories of their tango experiences and learning about the backgrounds of the people they met. As the night wore on, Laura found herself relaxing and enjoying the company of her new dance partners. She danced with men and women, old and young, all of them bringing their unique style and energy to the dance floor. She noticed the different styles of tango they danced, some more traditional while others were modern and experimental.

Laura sat at the table, catching her breath after her many dances, when she noticed a strange man enter the dance hall. He was tall and muscular, with a rugged look about him that sent a shiver down her spine. She noticed how his eyes roamed over the dancers as if he were searching for something. His intense gaze made her uneasy, and she could not shake the feeling that he was watching her too.

5. STRANGER

In the warm, inviting atmosphere of the milonga, where flickering candlelight danced on the walls, and harmonious tango tunes filled the air, the stranger seemed like an outlier. He navigated the crowd with decisive steps, his tall, slender frame gliding through the sea of dancers, his penetrating eyes scanning the room as if seeking someone or something. Laura couldn't help but feel a slight sense of discomfort in his presence. Her intuition had always been her reliable compass, steering her away from danger. However, this man triggered all her internal alarms.

As the night unfolded, the man remained a constant presence in the milonga, observing and lingering, akin to a watchful guardian or a predator biding its time. Laura couldn't dispel the unease that seemed to follow her around the room, a perpetual shadow she couldn't evade.

Just as she was about to leave, the man gently tapped her shoulder. She turned to see him standing before her, his gaze meeting hers with an intensity that made her heart race. "May I have this dance?" he asked in a low, gravelly voice that seemed to resonate within her core.

Laura hesitated, her mind awash with conflicting thoughts and fears. Something about him drew her in. She took his hand, and together they stepped onto the dance floor. This man was unlike anyone she had ever danced with before - powerful, magnetic, and enigmatic.

As they began to dance, Laura felt a good connection between them. Their steps were precise and deliberate, the rhythm of the tango guiding their movements. The man led confidently, his hand firm on her waist, while Laura followed his lead, her body responding instinctively to his cues. Their eyes locked as they navigated the dance floor, and Laura could sense a silent dialog forming between them.

The other dancers around them seemed to fade into the background as Laura and the stranger focused on their connection. Their movements were fluid, each step seamlessly transitioning into the next. The music pulsed, driving the dance forward and creating a sense of unity between them.

As they made their way back to the table, Laura felt anticipation blossoming inside of her. She couldn't help but feel drawn to this fascinating and mysterious man, pondering what secrets he might hold and what he might have in store for her.

After introducing himself as David, a distinguished professor of anthropology from an out-of-state university attending a conference in town, they engaged in a lively conversation about their mutual love of tango and their experiences dancing in various parts of the world. David regaled her with stories of his travels and the people he had met along the way, his words painting vibrant images.

Laura found herself becoming more and more intrigued by David, captivated by the way he talked and moved. She felt a surge of excitement building inside her, a feeling she hadn't experienced in a long time, as if a dormant ember within her soul had been reignited.

As they prepared to leave the milonga, David leaned in close and whispered in Laura's ear, his breath warm against her skin, "I have something new and exciting to show you. It's called Dancing with God."

Laura was taken aback by the mention of such a dance. "What is that?" she asked, her curiosity piqued.

David's smile was enigmatic and alluring. "It's a dance that has been passed down for generations from the ancient tribes. It's said to connect you with the divine, to channel the energy of the cosmos through your body."

Laura felt a jolt of curiosity and wonder. She had always been drawn to the mystical and spiritual, and the idea of a dance that could connect her with the divine sounded fascinating and irresistible.

"I'm in," she said eagerly, her eyes alight with anticipation. "Where do we go to learn this dance?"

David's eyes sparkled with mischief and excitement. "I know just the place. It is a secret dance hall, hidden from prying eyes, known only to a select few. It's where the true masters of Dancing with God go to hone their skills and unlock their inner power."

He continued, his voice brimming with enthusiasm and reverence, "This sacred dance originated in the ancient tribes of Mehri, nestled within the remote mountains. These tribes believed in the power of dance as a way to communicate with the divine and maintain a harmonious balance between the physical and spiritual realms. The Mehri people spent their lives mastering this dance, perfecting its intricate and fluid movements, which they believed would allow them to channel divine energy and awaken their inner power."

David paused for a moment, allowing the history of the dance to sink in, before continuing, "Over the centuries, the knowledge of this dance was passed down through generations, crossing borders and cultural barriers. The dance adapted and evolved, yet its essence remained unchanged – a profound connection with the divine, the ability to tap into the energy of the universe."

He leaned in closer, his voice barely above a whisper, "The select few who have mastered this dance are said to experience a transcendent state, a oneness with the cosmos as if they have become vessels for the divine to flow through. These dancers dedicate their lives to preserving the purity and power of Dancing with God, ensuring that its ancient wisdom is not lost to the sands of time."

David's words painted a vivid picture of the sacred dance, its origins steeped in mystery and reverence, and its profound impact on those fortunate enough to learn its secrets. The idea of experiencing a connection with the divine through dance ignited a fire within Laura, a burning desire to explore this mystical art form and unlock her hidden potential.

Filled with a sense of adventure and a renewed passion for life, Laura agreed to accompany David to this hidden jewel. As they stepped out of the milonga and into the cool night air, the city lights shimmered like a celestial map guiding their way. David hailed a taxi, and Laura couldn't help but wonder what lay ahead, her heart pounding with excitement and apprehension.

6.

WRITTEN STATEMENT

(Burnett County Police Files. Record #2.506/a)

July 8, 2020

Deputy Chief William Kopecky

Falls Park Police Precinct

Falls Park, NC 29778

Dear Officer,

I'm writing because I'm worried about my friend Laura Sommers. We've been close friends for a long time, and we usually talk and see each other a lot during the week. But lately, I can't reach her. She's not answering her phone or messages, and she's not opening her apartment door.

Laura is a very responsible person, and she's always quick to reply to my messages and calls. So, I'm concerned about her sudden silence.

I've gone to her place a few times and knocked on her door, but nobody's answering. I also talked to her neighbors, but they haven't seen her either.

I last saw Laura at a dance party at La Catedral. Laura loves to dance, especially the Argentine tango. She danced a lot that night, and I didn't see her when she left. Since then, I haven't heard from or seen her, and I'm scared for her safety.

Laura does not have a lot of close friends or family nearby, which makes me even more worried. I know she's been stressed lately, and I'm afraid something terrible might have happened. I've tried to think of why she might be gone, but I can't come up with anything. Laura is such a kind person, and I can't imagine anyone wanting to hurt her.

I'm asking if you could please look into this and see if you can find Laura. Any information you can give me would mean a lot, and I'll do whatever it takes to ensure she's okay. I'll also help with the investigation in any way I can.

If you need any more information from me or if I can help in any way, please let me know. I just want Laura to be safe.

Thank you for taking the time to read my letter.

Sincerely,

Susan Donnay

114 Aloma Ave. #120

Falls Park, NC 29708

7.

GRAY'S HAPPY BAR

Bartender Billy Gray, a tall man in his mid-forties with a trimmed beard and a contagious smile, wore a casual button-down shirt and jeans as he wiped down the counter. The bar was dimly lit, with a warm ambiance that attracted its loyal patrons. He greeted his regular, Chuck Gardner, who wore a worn-out baseball cap and a plaid shirt. Chuck was a burly man in his early fifties with a kind face and a booming laugh. "Hey there, Chuck, your usual Cuba Libre coming right up."

"Thanks, Billy; it's always good to see you. But, man, it's been a hot one today," Chuck said as he settled into his favorite stool near the corner of the bar.

"You're not wrong, Chuck. It's been sweltering all day. Makes you wonder what the rest of the summer is going to be like," Billy said, sweat beading on his forehead as the ceiling fan above them lazily spun.

"Yeah, it's brutal. Speaking of tough times, did you see those police cars outside the apartment building down the block?" Chuck asked.

"I did. You think they finally caught Hugh Lohman?" Billy asked, his eyes wide with curiosity as he placed a coaster down and set Chuck's drink on it.

"Could be, but you never know. Maybe it was something else. Maybe it was the Martinez family having another one of their infamous fights," Chuck said, shaking his head as he recalled their previous encounters with the law.

"You might be right, Chuck. I hear Sandra Martinez called the cops on her husband again," Billy said.

"That's just awful. That poor woman has five kids to care for, and she can't even count on her husband to be there for them," Chuck responded, swirling the ice cubes in his glass.

"Yeah, it's a tough situation. But what can you do? People must make their own choices," Billy said, shrugging his broad shoulders as he moved down the bar to serve another customer.

"I know, but sometimes those choices can have really bad consequences," Chuck noted.

Billy returned to Chuck, nodding in agreement. "That's true, Chuck. Here's to hoping things get better for everyone," Billy said, raising his glass in a toast.

"Agreed, Billy. Another Cuba Libre, please?" Chuck said, his spirits lifting slightly as he finished his first drink.

"Coming right up, Chuck," Billy said, mixing the drink with practiced ease, ice clinking against the glass.

"Hey, Billy, you've been running this bar for what, ten years now?" Chuck asked, leaning against the counter, and admiring the various bottles of liquor lining the shelves.

"That's right, Chuck. Ten long years," Billy said, sliding the drink across the counter to Chuck with a proud smile.

"You must have seen some crazy stuff during that time," Chuck said, sipping his drink as he glanced around the room, noting the eclectic mix of patrons.

"You have no idea, Chuck. I've seen it all. Fights, breakups, makeups, you name it," Billy said, a nostalgic glint in his eyes as he remembered some of the more memorable moments.

"What's the craziest thing you've ever seen?"

"Well, there was this one time when this guy walked in and ordered a drink. He seemed like a normal guy, but after a while, he started talking to himself, and then he just fell off his chair," Billy said, chuckling at the memory.

"Wow, that's wild. What did you do?"

"I called an ambulance, of course. You never know what is going to happen in this business," Billy said, shaking his head.

"Speaking of crazy stuff, Billy, have you heard rumors about a person disappearing in the neighborhood?" Chuck asked, his tone serious as he thought about the recent chatter amongst his neighbors.

"No, I haven't. So who are you talking about?" Billy asked, concern furrowing his brow and placing the clean glass on the shelf.

"I heard from my neighbor that someone has gone missing recently. Do you think the police activity could be related to that?" Chuck took a nice sip of his drink.

Billy pursed his lips thoughtfully before responding, "It's possible, Chuck. I hope they find whoever is missing and that everything turns out okay."

Chuck nodded in agreement, "Yeah, me too. It's a scary thought that something like that could happen around here."

Billy placed a comforting hand on Chuck's shoulder, "Definitely. But let's try not to dwell on the negative. Here's another drink, Chuck. Enjoy!"

The two men continued chatting, sharing stories and laughter, as the evening wore on. The lively atmosphere of Gray's Happy Bar provided a welcome escape from the worries and challenges of everyday life. For a few hours, they could enjoy each other's company and the familiar routine of idle conversations. As the bartender expertly mixed cocktails and Chuck nursed his favorite drink, they exchanged observations about the various patrons, reminisced about memorable events that had taken place within the bar's walls, and discussed the latest local news.

8. FACEBOOK GROUP CHAT

Tango Enthusiasts United (1.0K members)

Maria Rogan posted: Hey, has anyone heard from Susan Donnay or knows what's up with Laura Sommers? I heard Susan contacted the police.

Top comments:

Jan Salas — I haven't heard anything. What happened?

Fran Mowley — Yeah, I'm out of the loop too. Does anyone know what's going on?

Miriam Uri — Sorry, I'm clueless.

Bob Kane — No idea, but I hope everything is okay.

Megan Dwyer — Same. Sending good vibes, just in case.

Katya Pulemo	Hoping for the best.
Donna Simmons	I haven't heard anything either.
Paula Norwood	This is news to me. I hope Laura is okay.
Eric Larson	Nope, no idea. But now I'm concerned.
Ken King	I hope they find her soon.
Fran Mowley	Super concerned. Please keep us updated, Maria.
Gretel Guido	Absolutely. Let us know if we can help in any way.
Bob Kane	Sending prayers for Laura and her family.
Megan Dwyer	I hope Susan gets some answers soon.
Tara Simmons	Let's hope for the best.
Paula Norwood	If anyone hears anything, please update us.
Eric Larson	I'm here if anyone needs support or help.
Ken King	Let's all hope and pray for Laura's safe return.
Jan Salas	On a lighter note, who's attending the practica tonight?
Megan Dwyer	Jan Salas, did you find my shoes?
Scott Lea	I'll be there tonight; excited to see everyone!
Vanessa Klein	Can't wait to see you all, Rahul will be DJing!
Irene Kelly	I had no idea about Laura. Please keep us posted.
Rita Thompson	Lighting a candle for Laura.

Barb Castro	I hope everything turns out okay. Stay strong, everyone.
Josh Patel	Fingers crossed for good news.
Steve Kim	Let's stay positive and hope for the best.
Valery Fargo	It's such a tight-knit community. We'll support each other through this.
Anna Chen	We should organize a search party if needed.
Milena Ross	Great idea, Anna. Count me in.
Nick Archer	I'll be there too. We need to support each other.
Augusto Kirin	If there's anything I can do, just let me know.
Jan Salas	Megan, I didn't find your shoes. Maybe someone else picked them up?

9.
SERGEANT RAE

Date: July 9, 2020

Time: 10:00 AM

To: Deputy Chief William Kopecky, Falls Park Police Precinct

Re: Report on Investigation into the Disappearance of Laura Sommers

Deputy Chief:

I am writing to report on my recent investigation into the disappearance of Laura Sommers, the young woman who was reported missing last week. Following your orders, I paid a visit to the apartment house where Laura lived and made some inquiries.

Upon arrival at the house, I found the apartment empty, with no response to my knocks. I observed that the mailbox was stuffed with unopened mail, indicating that the apartment had been vacant for some time. I then proceeded to talk to several neighbors, hoping to obtain some helpful information.

Unfortunately, Ms. Sommers was a private individual who rarely talked about her life with neighbors, so the first few inquiries yielded nothing useful. Finally, however, I was fortunate to speak with Mrs. Fielding, an older lady who lived on the first floor. Mrs. Fielding informed me that she knew Laura well and that the last time she saw her was at about 8 pm on Tuesday, the day of Laura's disappearance.

Mrs. Fielding stated that Laura was in high spirits that day and was dressed in an elegant outfit, indicating that she was going to the La Catedral dance hall, where she frequently dances the Argentine tango. Mrs. Fielding also stated that she did not see Laura coming back home that night, as she usually sits at her window and watches people who come and go from the building—Mrs. Fielding's sleepless nights often kept her up late, which gave her a clear view of the building entrance.

During my investigation, I also spoke with the building's maintenance man, Mr. Monadi, who mentioned that he didn't notice anything unusual or out of place in the days leading up to Laura's disappearance. He did, however, mention that Laura seemed preoccupied and more reserved than usual in the last few days before she went missing.

I then went to La Catedral dance hall, where I spoke with the staff and some regular patrons. Many remembered Laura as an enthusiastic dancer and a friendly person. Still, no one had any helpful information about her whereabouts or what might have happened to her on the night she disappeared.

In light of these findings, I recommend that we conduct further investigations, including checking Laura's phone records and CCTV footage around the La Catedral dance hall and interviewing any individuals who may have had contact with her on the day of her disappearance. We should also consider contacting her family and close friends to determine if they have any insight into her current state of mind or any potential reasons for her sudden disappearance.

I will continue to follow up on any leads in this case, and I will keep you informed of any progress.

Respectfully,

Police Sergeant Leonard Rae

A handwritten note attached to the Police Sergeant's report:

"Hey Lenny, great report man! Listen, we found some surveillance video from the day that girl went missing. It turns out there was a distinctive taxi, a 2019 Corolla with the license plate TB-2965, that picked up two passengers at the La Catedral dance hall around midnight. Can you do me a favor and track down the driver? Let's see if he can give us any info. Thanks, man. William."

10.
CAB DRIVER SINGH

To: Deputy Chief Kopecky

Date: July 13, 2020

Sir,

I am forwarding this transcript of the audio recording of the interview I conducted last Friday with cab driver Anand Singh. The interview appeared to go well, and Mr. Singh sounded truthful in providing the facts regarding the ride he gave to Laura Sommers and her companion.

However, there is one very unusual detail that has come to light. The address Mr. Singh mentions in his testimony, 1900 Forest Hills Dr., does indeed exist. However, upon further investigation, we discovered that there is neither a church nor any other building at this address. In fact, it is a piece of abandoned land belonging to the city, which has never had any construction on it. The site is nothing more than a local dump with trash scattered everywhere.

In light of this information, we may need to interrogate Mr. Singh in greater detail, as there might be more to the story than he initially revealed. Additionally, I strongly recommend contacting the local FBI office to seek their assistance and expertise, as the case is becoming increasingly complex.

Please find for your review the attached transcript (Document 16) of my interview with the driver Anand Singh. Let me know if you have further questions or recommendations for the next steps.

Sincerely,

Police Sergeant Leonard Rae

Document 16.

Falls Park Police Precinct

Interview Room 2

Date: July 10, 2020

Time: 2:30 PM

Interviewer: Police Sergeant Rae

Witness: Anand Singh

[BEGIN TRANSCRIPT]

Sergeant Rae: All right, Mr. Singh, let's start with the basics. Can you please state your full name for the record?

Anand Singh: My name is Anand Singh.

Sergeant Rae: Thank you, Mr. Singh. Now, we understand you're a Yellow Cab company cab driver driving a Toyota Corolla. We want to ask you about a particular ride on Tuesday, June 30th. Do you remember picking up a couple at the La Catedral dance hall entrance at around midnight?

Anand Singh: Yes, I remember that ride. The woman was in her 30s, wearing a red dress. She had long, dark hair and seemed excited about something. I can't quite remember how her companion looked, however. He was taller than her and wore a dark suit, but I did not get a good look at his face.

Sergeant Rae: Can you tell me where you drove them?

Anand Singh: They gave me the address 1900 Forest Hills Dr., on the outskirts of town. It's a bit secluded, with many trees and few houses around.

Sergeant Rae: Did you hear any conversation between the passengers during the 30-minute ride?

Anand Singh: They mainly talked quietly, so I couldn't catch everything. I do remember the woman mentioning that she hadn't been to a place like this before and her companion reassuring her that she would have a good time.

Sergeant Rae: Can you describe the location where you dropped them off?

Anand Singh: It was a lonely two-story brick building that looked like an old church. The windows were brightly lit, the building didn't appear to be abandoned. There was a gravel path leading up to the entrance, and no cars were parked nearby. The passengers paid their fare, gave me a nice tip, and went towards the building.

Sergeant Rae: What did you do after dropping them off?

Anand Singh: That was my last ride for the day, so I drove home and went to bed around 2 am.

Sergeant Rae: Is there anything else you can tell us about the passengers or the ride?

Anand Singh: When he paid me, I noticed the man had a distinctive ring on his right hand, with a large black stone. Other than that, there was nothing unusual about them, and I don't have anything else to add.

Sergeant Rae: Did you notice any other vehicles or people around when you dropped them off at the church building?

Anand Singh: Not that I recall. It was a quiet area, and I did not see anyone else around. I only remember the wind rustling through the trees.

Sergeant Rae: Did you notice anything about the woman that might suggest she was under duress or being coerced?

Anand Singh: No, she seemed to be in good spirits and showed no signs of distress. She was laughing and chatting with her companion, and they appeared to be getting along well.

Sergeant Rae: Did they ask you to wait for them or request a return trip?

Anand Singh: They didn't ask me to wait or mention anything about needing a ride back. They thanked me and walked towards the church after I dropped them off.

Sergeant Rae: All right, Mr. Singh, we appreciate your cooperation. We may have more questions for you later, so please stay in town for the next few days. We may need to call you in for another interview.

Anand Singh: Sure, no problem. I hope I have helped.

Sergeant Rae: Thank you, Mr. Singh. You've been very helpful. Is there anything else you can recall about that night that might be relevant to our investigation?

Anand Singh: Well, now that you mention it, I do remember hearing some music coming from the building where I dropped them off. It was faint, but I could make out the sound of a violin and a piano playing a slow melody. It struck me as a bit odd for an old church, but I didn't think much of it at the time.

Sergeant Rae: That's interesting. We'll look into that as well. If you remember anything else, please don't hesitate to contact us. Your assistance in this case is invaluable, and we appreciate your cooperation.

Anand Singh: You're welcome, officer.

[END OF TRANSCRIPT]

11.
FBI CASE #A764334

Source: Federal Bureau of Investigation

Subject: Request for FBI Assistance in Possible Abduction Case

Title: Letter from Deputy Police Chief William Kopecky

Publication Date: July 17, 2020

Category: Unclassified Correspondence

URL: [REDACTED]

17 July 2020

To: Javier Garcia, Special Agent in Charge
FBI Field Office

Dear Special Agent Garcia,

I am writing to request assistance from the Federal Bureau of Investigation in the ongoing investigation into the disappearance of a young woman, Laura Sommers, in our small town of Falls Park. Given the circumstances and our limited resources, we believe it would be in the best interest of the investigation to involve the FBI.

The incident occurred on June 30, 2020, and since then, our police department has been actively investigating the case. Unfortunately, despite our best efforts, we have been unable to identify any concrete leads, and the case remains unresolved. Due to the nature of the disappearance and the possibility of an abduction, we believe it is necessary to seek the expertise and resources of the FBI to help bring resolution to this case and ensure the safety of Ms. Sommers and our community.

Our department has gathered evidence and witness statements, which we are prepared to share with your agents to facilitate a smooth collaboration. We understand that the FBI has jurisdiction in matters involving the kidnapping or abduction of individuals, and we hope that your involvement will expedite the process of finding Ms. Sommers and bringing her home safely.

Please let us know the next steps for coordinating our efforts and how we can best assist your agents in this investigation. Our department is committed to working alongside the FBI to ensure a comprehensive investigation and a successful outcome for Ms. Sommers and her family.

Thank you for your prompt attention to this urgent matter. I look forward to your response and working together to solve this case.

Sincerely,

William Kopecky

Deputy Chief, Falls Park Police Precinct

Document 25 [UNCLASSIFIED]

July 18, 2020

To: Special Agent Thomas Bishop

Re: Assignment to Investigate Possible Abduction in Falls Park, NC
New Case Number: A764334

Thomas,

You have been assigned to investigate a possible abduction case in Falls Park, NC, as requested by the local police department. The case involves the unresolved disappearance of a young woman, and we believe our expertise and resources will be invaluable in ensuring her safety and resolving the case.

Please find the case details, including relevant evidence and witness statements, attached to this letter. Your primary objectives are to:

1. Establish and maintain communication with the city police department to coordinate efforts and facilitate information exchange.
2. Review the attached case details to identify potential leads.
3. Conduct additional interviews, gather further evidence, and perform other necessary investigative activities in collaboration with the local police department.
4. Provide regular updates to our field office and local law enforcement regarding the progress of the investigation.

As the lead agent on this case, you are authorized to utilize the necessary resources and personnel to ensure a thorough investigation. Your swift action and expertise are crucial to the resolution of this case.

Please proceed to Falls Park at your earliest convenience to begin the investigation. Should you require additional support or resources, do not hesitate to contact our field office.

Sincerely,

-SIGNATURE-

Javier Garcia

Special Agent in Charge

12.
THE DAILY BUZZ

Friday Edition, July 24, 2020

COMMUNITY UNITES IN RESPONSE TO THE MYSTERIOUS DISAPPEARANCE OF YOUNG WOMAN

By Liliana Winkler

Residents of Falls Park have been left stunned following the disappearance of Laura Sommers, a young woman who vanished without a trace three weeks ago. Despite a thorough investigation by local law enforcement and the FBI, there are still no leads on her whereabouts, leaving the community worried and confused.

As a reporter for The Daily Buzz, I have been closely following this case and had the opportunity to speak with FBI Special Agent Thomas Bishop, who has been assigned to investigate Laura's disappearance. During our conversation, Agent Bishop emphasized that the FBI is working tirelessly to find Laura and bring her home safely. However, he could not provide any specific details on the investigation, citing the need to maintain its integrity.

The lack of information has led to speculation and rumors in the community, causing additional stress and worry. Mayor John Gommels expressed his concern for the situation and reassured residents that the town is doing everything in its power to assist with the investigation. "We're working closely with law enforcement and the FBI to get to the bottom of what happened," Mayor Gommels said.

At the same time, tensions have risen among city council members as they debate the allocation of funds towards the investigation. Councilman Mateo Davis has criticized Mayor Gommels for not taking enough action and not providing sufficient resources for the investigation. "We need to be doing more to help find Laura and bring her home safely. The mayor needs to step up and show real leadership," Councilman Davis said.

Councilwoman Terri Coxwell, a member of the opposition party, has been particularly vocal in her criticism of the mayor. "It's clear that Mayor Gommels is more interested in protecting his political interests than in protecting the people of Falls Park," Coxwell said. "We need a leader who is willing to put the safety of our community first."

In response, Mayor Gommels has emphasized the need for caution and patience in handling the investigation. "We need to follow the proper procedures and protocols in order to ensure a thorough and accurate investigation. We will not rush this process and risk compromising its integrity," Mayor Gommels said.

Despite the political tensions, the community has rallied together to support one another during this difficult time. Many have organized candlelight vigils and posted flyers around town to raise awareness about Laura's disappearance. The outpouring of love and support has been heartening to see and has demonstrated the strength and resilience of our community. While rumors and theories continue to circulate, it's important to remain hopeful and trust in the ongoing efforts of law enforcement and the FBI.

Liliana Winkler

Reporter for The Daily Buzz

13.

SHEILA AND ABIGAIL

Sheila Fielding: "Abigail, you wouldn't believe who showed up at my door the other day. It was an FBI agent, Thomas Bishop. He came to ask about Laura from Apartment 11B. She's been missing for a month now."

Abigail Hoffman: "Oh my goodness! What did he want to know?"

Sheila: "Well, before we got into all of that, I have to tell you, Abigail, he was the most handsome agent I've ever seen! He was well-dressed too like he had just stepped out of a fashion magazine. So, naturally, I invited him in and offered him coffee and a slice of my famous chocolate Babka. I thought it would be a nice way to make him feel welcome and comfortable."

Abigail: "Oh, Sheila, always the gracious host. What happened next?"

Sheila: "As we sat down, he began asking about Laura. But before I could answer, I found myself telling him all about my late husband,

Colonel Joseph Fielding. You remember Joseph, don't you? He also was a very handsome man, an Iraq war veteran. I just went on about how much Joseph loved my cooking, especially my chocolate Babka. I even mentioned how he and I would have these lovely Sunday dinners together, where I would prepare his favorite dishes."

Abigail: "That sounds so like you, Sheila. So, what did you end up telling Agent Bishop about Laura?"

Sheila: "Oh, right! Well, as we continued talking, I couldn't help but ask if Agent Bishop was married. Can you believe he's still single? I told him so many good-looking women would love to be his wife. But he said his job was his main focus right now. He even shared some stories about his work with the FBI, though he couldn't reveal too many details, of course. Anyway, after our little chit-chat, we finally got around to discussing Laura."

Abigail: "And what did you tell him?"

Sheila: "I told him that Laura was a quiet, reclusive girl who mostly kept to herself. She didn't have any loud parties or cause any trouble. But she was an avid dancer, you see. She loved to dance the Argentine tango and would go dancing every week. I also mentioned how she seemed very dedicated to her dancing practice, as she'd often leave her apartment with her dance shoes in hand."

Abigail: "Interesting. What else did you say?"

Sheila: "Well, talking about dancing reminded me of my younger days when I used to dance the waltz. I was quite a dancer back then, Abigail. Men would practically fight to dance with me! But, of course, all of that was before I married Joseph. He was so jealous, you know. He wouldn't let me dance with anyone but him. Oh, how I miss those days. I even showed Agent Bishop some old photographs of Joseph and me at various dance events."

Abigail: "I remember you telling me about that, Sheila. But what about Laura? Did you tell Agent Bishop anything else about her?"

Sheila: "Yes, I did. On the day she disappeared, I happened to see Laura as she was leaving her apartment. She seemed to be in a hurry and told me she was going to a dance hall. That was the last time I saw her. I also mentioned that she had a few close friends in the dance community, but I didn't know much about them, unfortunately."

Abigail: "Oh, how dreadful! Did Agent Bishop have any clues or ideas about what could have happened to her?"

Sheila: "He didn't say much, but I could tell he took everything I said seriously. He asked a few more questions about Laura's friends and if she had any enemies, but I really couldn't give him much more information than I already had. I just hope they find her, Abigail. She was such a sweet girl."

Abigail: "I hope so too, Sheila. I'm glad you were able to provide the FBI with some information. Who knows, it might just help solve the case."

Sheila: "Oh, I almost forgot! Agent Bishop asked if Laura had any romantic interests or was seeing someone. I told him I wasn't sure, but I had seen her with a gentleman a few times, someone I didn't recognize. They seemed close, but I didn't want to pry."

Abigail: "That could be important information, Sheila. Did Agent Bishop say what their next steps would be?"

Sheila: "He mentioned that they were looking into all possible leads and trying to find connections between Laura's disappearance and her personal life. They would also interview some of her friends from the dance community to see if they knew anything."

Abigail: "It sounds like they're doing everything possible to find her. I'll be praying for her safe return."

Sheila: "Thank you, Abigail. I appreciate that. It's unsettling to think that something like this could happen so close to home. But, it reminds us to cherish every moment we have with our loved ones."

Abigail: "You're right. I will call my daughter right now and tell her how much I love her. You never know what the future holds."

Sheila: "That's a lovely idea. Times like these make us realize how important family and friends are."

Abigail: "Absolutely, Sheila."

14. BISHOP TO GARCIA (PHONE CALL)

[START TRANSCRIPT]

Thomas Bishop: "Hello. Good morning, sir. Special Agent Bishop calling from Falls Park on an open line."

SAC Javier Garcia: "Good morning, Tom. How's the investigation going?"

Bishop: "Well, it's been four weeks since Laura Sommers disappeared, and we still don't have any significant leads. I've been conducting interviews with Laura's neighbors, her close friend Susan Donnay, and members of the local tango group she was a part of. However, despite my efforts, I haven't found any actionable information. I'm starting to feel a bit desperate."

Garcia: "I understand your frustration, Tom. These cases can be incredibly challenging. What about forensic analysis? Have you found any evidence at the scene or in her home?"

Bishop: "We've processed the scene thoroughly, and we've also searched Laura's home. However, we haven't found anything that could lead us to a suspect or provide a motive for the disappearance."

Garcia: "How about the community? Are they cooperating with the investigation?"

Bishop: "Yes, the community has been very supportive. They've organized search parties and have been helping us distribute flyers and posters around town. But, unfortunately, we still haven't received any tips that could lead us to her whereabouts."

Garcia: "I see. Now, you mentioned that you hadn't found any significant leads. Is there anything that's caught your attention or seemed unusual?"

Bishop: "Actually, there is one thing that's been bothering me. The cab driver's testimony said he dropped off Laura and her companion near a building that night. The problem is, there's no building there, and there has never been. So it doesn't make any sense."

Garcia: "That is odd. Have you considered the possibility that the cab driver is mistaken or hiding something?"

Bishop: "Yes, I have. At this point, he seems to be our only lead, even if it's a minor one. I request authorization to conduct a polygraph test on the driver to see if we can resolve this discrepancy."

Garcia: "Given the circumstances, I think that's a reasonable request. You have my authorization to proceed with the polygraph test. Remember that polygraph results are not always conclusive, so continue pursuing other leads as well."

Bishop: "Understood, sir. I appreciate your support. I'll schedule the polygraph test soon and continue looking for other leads. I won't rest until we find Laura."

Garcia: "I know you won't, Tom. Just remember that you have the full support of the Bureau behind you. If you need anything, don't hesitate to reach out."

Bishop: "Thank you, sir. I'll keep you informed of any significant developments or breakthroughs in the investigation."

Garcia: "I look forward to hearing from you, Tom. Stay focused and stay safe out there. And remember, we're all working together to bring Laura home."

Bishop: "Thank you, sir. I'll do my best."

[END OF TRANSCRIPT]

15.
POLYGRAPH TEST REPORT

Subject: Anand Singh (Cab Driver)

Examiner: Special Agent Thomas Bishop, Federal Bureau of Investigation

Date of Examination: Wednesday, July 29, 2020

Purpose of Examination:

The purpose of this polygraph examination is to determine the truthfulness of Anand Singh's statement regarding the transportation of a young woman and her companion to a specific building on June 30, 2020.

Background:

Anand Singh, a cab driver working for the Yellow Cab Company, claims to have picked up a young woman and her companion from a dancing hall at about midnight on June 30, 2020, and transported them to a building located at 1900 Forest Hills Dr. Special Agent Thomas

Bishop administered a polygraph examination to verify the accuracy of Mr. Singh's statement.

Pre-Test Interview:

During the pre-test interview, Anand Singh was informed of the examination procedure, his rights, and the nature of the questions that would be asked. Mr. Singh provided consent to participate in the polygraph examination.

Relevant Questions and Responses:

Question: Is your name Anand Singh?

Response: Yes

Question: Were you born on April 4, 1985, in Chandigarh, province of Punjab, India?

Response: Yes

Question: Are you currently employed as a cab driver with the Yellow Cab Company?

Response: Yes

Question: Do you have a girlfriend named Anisha Kaur?

Response: Yes

Question: At about midnight on June 30, 2020, did you pick up a young woman and her companion from a dancing hall?

Response: Yes

Question: Did the passengers provide the destination address as 1900 Forest Hills Dr.?

Response: Yes

Question: Did both passengers leave the cab and enter a two-story building at the provided address?

Response: Yes

Question: Have you seen the passengers since that night?

Response: No

Question: Are you familiar with the building or the surrounding area of 1900 Forest Hills Dr.?

Response: No

Question: Have you intentionally withheld any information related to the transportation of the young woman and her companion?

Response: No

Polygraph Results:

The polygraph examination results indicate that Anand Singh's responses to the relevant questions were consistent with truthful answers. In addition, no significant physiological reactions indicative of deception were detected during the examination.

Conclusion:

Based on the results of the polygraph examination, it appears that Anand Singh was truthful when stating that he picked up the young woman and her companion from a dancing hall on June 30, 2020, and transported them to the building located at 1900 Forest Hills Dr. as described in his statement.

16.

GARCIA TO BISHOP

DATE: August 7, 2020

TO: Special Agent Thomas Bishop, FD00983

FROM: SAC Javier Garcia

SUBJECT: Memo from Falls Park City Council - Laura Sommers Case

SENT VIA: [EMAIL ADDRESS REDACTED]

Tom,

I have contacted the Falls Park City Council through our official channels. I requested a memo about the location where Laura Sommers was last seen and any known details about that area from the city's perspective.

I have received a response from the city planner, which I have included in this email. While I don't believe the information provided offers any direct clues to help solve the case, it may still be useful in our ongoing investigation. Therefore, I recommend you carefully review the memo, as it might offer new angles or insights to pursue.

As you know, sometimes even the smallest information can lead to a breakthrough in a case. Therefore, please consider the contents of this memo in the context of our investigation and explore any possible connections or leads that may arise from it.

Please keep me updated on your progress, and don't hesitate to reach out if you require further assistance or resources. We are committed to solving this case and bringing Laura Sommers home.

Best regards,

SAC Garcia

[ATTACHMENT: LETTER FROM CITY COUNCIL]

Subject: Explanation Regarding Unused City-Owned Land Lot

August 4, 2020

To Whom It May Concern

I am responding to the inquiry about the city-owned land lot at 1900 Forest Hills Drive. As a City Planner for the Falls Park Planning and Development Department, I oversee land use, zoning, and development within the city.

The land lot in question has a unique history contributing to its current unused state. Our records do not indicate any previous ownership; the city has owned the lot for an extended period.

The primary factor contributing to the lot remaining undeveloped is soil contamination due to elevated levels of mercury. The presence of mercury in the soil poses significant environmental and health risks. As a result, potential developers have hesitated to invest in the property because remediating the soil contamination would require extensive effort, resulting in significant costs and delays. Additionally, the lot's environmental constraints may limit the types of developments that can be built on the site, further reducing developer interest.

Our department is aware of the concerns regarding the unused land lot and is actively exploring options for its future development. The town's potential plans for environmental remediation on this lot include:

1. Conducting a comprehensive environmental assessment to determine the extent and nature of the mercury contamination in the soil.
2. Developing a remediation plan to address the contamination may involve methods such as excavation, stabilization, or in situ treatment.
3. Collaborating with environmental agencies and experts to ensure the remediation plan complies with regulations and best practices for managing mercury contamination.
4. Seeking funding opportunities, such as grants or partnerships, to assist with covering the costs of the remediation efforts.
5. Once the site is deemed safe for development, work with developers to create a sustainable and community-oriented project that aligns with the city's long-term vision.

Please feel free to reach out if you have any further questions or concerns about this land lot or other city planning and development matters. We appreciate your interest in our city's growth and development.

Paul H. Truran, City Planner

Falls Park Planning and Development Department

17.
BISHOP TO GARCIA

DATE: August 10, 2020

TO: SAC Javier Garcia

FROM: Special Agent Thomas Bishop, FD00983

SUBJECT: Request for Guidance

SENT VIA EMAIL: [REDACTED]

Dear SAC Garcia,

Thank you very much for the memo from the Falls Park City Council. As you suggested, this information only helps a little in the investigation. In fact, it further complicates the case by presenting contradictory evidence, which only deepens the mystery and leaves me both frustrated and disheartened.

As you know, I subjected the driver who transported Laura Sommers and an unidentified male companion to the address at 1900 Forest Hills Drive to a polygraph test authorized by you. The driver passed the test, fully corroborating his testimony. If you recall, sir, that night the driver claims to have witnessed the couple enter a two-story building resembling a church, complete with illuminated windows and soft music emanating from within.

Yet my conversations with local residents, as well as the memo from the town planner you sent, paint a vastly different picture. No such building exists at the specified address, and it never has! This stark contrast between the driver's account and the information I have gathered from other sources has left me bewildered and questioning my judgment.

To maintain my sanity and seek some semblance of clarity, I personally visited the location in question. As I stood on the empty lot, surrounded by ancient trees and littered with scattered garbage, I couldn't shake the feeling that something wasn't quite right. The inexplicable nature of the driver's account weighed heavily on me, and I found myself consumed by an overwhelming sense of unease. Yet, despite the apparent lack of concrete evidence, a nagging intuition told me that this baffling discrepancy could be the key to unlocking the truth behind Ms. Sommers' disappearance.

I remembered, sir, that you once told me a good investigator when out of factual evidence, has to rely on gut feeling. And so, I did. I started to search for similar cases of people disappearing in this town. I browsed through old police records and interviewed at least a dozen people with no apparent success. I was so disappointed that I nearly abandoned my research until I encountered a fascinating gentleman whose story instantly captured my attention. I need to report to you about it.

The gentleman's name is Edmund Drake. In the conversation with me, this retired high school teacher in his early 80s, reminisced about his youth when he and his girlfriend were part of a local hippie commune. This tight-knit group of individuals embraced values of peace, love, and harmony, living together in a makeshift campsite. They frequently gathered around bonfires to share stories, play music, and partake in spiritual practices. Mr. Drake mentioned that several commune members were especially intrigued by a mystical ritual called "Dancing with God."

Each night after midnight, they would form a circle and dance to an enigmatic melody played on a tape recorder. Their graceful, sensuous movements, in sync with the music, captivated the rest of the commune, who delighted in watching this mesmerizing performance.

However, one fateful morning, all 12 dancers—young men and women—mysteriously vanished. No one could fathom why they had left or where they had gone. They just disappeared, leaving all their belongings behind at the camp. The town was abuzz with speculation, wondering how this group could vanish without leaving any note or trace. As years passed, the strange event faded from people's memory, Mr. Drake told me.

The connection between the enigmatic event recounted by Edmund Drake and Laura Sommers' disappearance has left me both captivated and deeply troubled. Is there a concealed link between these seemingly unrelated incidents? I am growing increasingly convinced that the key to unraveling Laura Sommers' disappearance lies in exposing the truth behind these peculiar events from the past.

I have delved further into the history of the town and its surrounding area. I have consulted local historians and explored the police archives, seeking any information that could illuminate these unexplainable occurrences. My thorough research has unearthed several additional cases of disappearances spanning decades.

Intriguingly, all these cases seem to share a common thread: each individual vanished not far from the same area where the alleged "church" building was described by the taxi driver. This pattern of disappearances, combined with the driver's seemingly impossible account, only fuel my growing conviction that there is more to this case than meets the eye. I can't shake the feeling that a hidden truth lurks just beneath the surface, waiting to be uncovered.

I now find myself grappling with questions that seem to defy logic and reason. How can a building described in such vivid detail by the cab driver not exist? Is there something about the area that has led to the unexplained disappearances of several people over the years?

As I continue my pursuit of answers, I cannot help but feel that I am venturing into uncharted territory. The twists and turns of this investigation have left me feeling disoriented and uncertain of the path ahead. In moments like these, I am grateful for your guidance and support.

I eagerly await your response and any advice or suggestions you may have regarding our next steps. I am determined to solve this case and ensure that Laura Sommers and the countless others who have vanished are not forgotten.

Sincerely,

Special Agent Thomas Bishop

18.
RESIGNATION

DATE: August 19, 2020

TO: SAC Javier Garcia

FROM: Special Agent Thomas Bishop, FD00983

SUBJECT: Resignation

SENT VIA EMAIL: [REDACTED]

Sir,

With a heavy heart, I must inform you that I am submitting my immediate resignation as a Special Agent. During my ten years at the Bureau, I have acquired invaluable knowledge and am thankful to have worked with such exceptional colleagues under your guidance. The experience and investigative skills I've gained will forever be treasured.

The Laura Sommers case has profoundly affected my mental and physical health. The investigation is filled with dead ends and enigmatic puzzles that I have never faced in my career. I've spent countless sleepless nights examining the details, searching for elusive answers.

Though I'm not a superstitious person, I can't help but feel as if something or someone is deliberately leading me astray in this case.

My apprehensions have only grown with recent, inexplicable development.

You may find this as shocking as I did just two days ago, but it seems that Laura Sommers might not have been abducted at all. Surprisingly, she appears to be alive and well, as her best friend Susan Donnay received a phone call from Laura herself! Can you imagine, sir?

Before you dismiss the abduction case, let me describe everything in detail as it transpired. On Monday, August 17, I received a phone call from Susan Donnay, whom I had interviewed several times. Her voice was quivering, and she sounded deeply unsettled. She informed me that Laura had called her, saying she was pretty content with her situation and had no desire to return home. Although Laura's voice seemed calm and happy, she wouldn't reveal her location, how she ended there, or why she had been missing for a long time. I cannot exclude the possibility that Laura was speaking from a captive state, perhaps under the influence of drugs or in another distressing situation.

I promptly asked Ms. Donnay to document her conversation with Laura, including as many details as she could recall. I am attaching the transcript of their conversation to this email. I advise that you scrutinize it meticulously, as it may contain clues that I have not been able to detect. I also propose tracing the call from Laura to determine its origin using our ____ [REDACTED].

As for myself, I must regard my participation in this case as concluded. The emotional burden of the investigation has become intolerable, and I worry that continuing to work on it will only further endanger my well-being.

Another contributing factor to my decision to resign is the recent decline in my health. Over the past three weeks, I have experienced a steady deterioration in my overall well-being, marked by symptoms such as constant fatigue, unrelenting headaches, and unexplained weight loss. As a result, doctors have recommended comprehensive medical examinations to identify the cause of my issues. Unfortunately, these tests will demand significant time and energy, rendering it impossible for me to continue working for the foreseeable future.

I apologize for any inconvenience this may cause and hope a more adept investigator can be assigned to this case. I trust that my successor will be able to navigate the intricacies of this case more effectively than I have been. Thank you for your understanding and support. I am deeply grateful for the opportunities I have been granted as a Special Agent, and I will always cherish the experiences and friendships I have forged along the way. Please guide me on proceeding with my resignation and any necessary documentation.

Sincerely,

Special Agent Thomas Bishop

[TRANSCRIPT OF A PHONE CALL FROM LAURA SOMMERS]

[DATE: AUGUST 17, 2020]

[TIME: APPR. 9AM]

Susan Donnay: "Hello?"

Laura Sommers: "Hi, Susan."

Susan: "Laura? Oh my god, where are you? Are you okay?"

Laura: "I'm fine, Susan. I'm sorry I had to call you like this."

Susan: "What's going on, Laura? Where are you?"

Laura: "I'm not sure how to explain it. The world is beautiful. Lush hills and a bright sky. Crisp air. It's tranquil here."

Susan: "Laura, I don't understand. How did you call me? And where are you?"

Laura: "I can't describe it, Susan. I don't know how it worked, but I had to contact you. I don't want to leave this place. I feel like I belong here more than I do at home."

Susan: "Laura, what do you mean? You can't just vanish like that. Everyone is worried sick about you. And the police have been questioning me about you."

Laura: "I know it, and I'm sorry. I just had to let you know that I'm okay. I don't want you to worry about me anymore."

Susan: "Laura, please come back. We miss you. We need you."

Laura: "I'm sorry, Susan. I can't come back right now. I will stay here. And I feel fantastic."

Susan: "Laura, please tell me where you are. I'll come and get you."

Laura: "I won't be able to tell you, Susan. And I do not know how you can get here. I just wanted to call and say that I'm content and much wiser now. I understood many things about music and dancing that never occurred before."

Susan: "Laura, please come back. You're frightening me. I don't know what to do."

Laura: "I'm sorry, Susan. I must go now. Please tell everyone I'm okay. I won't be calling anymore; you can't imagine the distance. I love you."

[END OF TRANSCRIPT]

19.

FALLS PARK CITY ARCHIVE

August 21, 2020

Curator, Falls Park City Archive

Subject: 19th Century Document Research Findings

Dear Curator,

I am writing to share the results of my recent research in the municipal archive's 19th-century document collection. While conducting research on behalf of a patron (requested by Special Agent Thomas Bishop), I came across a fascinating and mysterious note penned in 1854 by the local priest, Father Damian Francis, in his personal diary. This entry sheds light on some perplexing happenings in our town's history, which may be relevant to the current investigation.

I have made a photocopy of the page and added it to the archive's catalog under the appropriate document reference number to assist future researchers in locating and utilizing the valuable primary resource. I have also taken the initiative to include a copy of this intriguing note from Father Damian's diary in this email. I believe it may be of particular interest to Agent Bishop or anyone else invested in the investigation.

Please feel free to contact me should you require any further information or assistance in deciphering the historical significance and context of the diary entry. I remain at your disposal.

Sincerely,

John Levi, Reference Librarian

[Attachment: Diary_Entry_1854_Father_Damian.pdf]

11th November, 1854

It is with a burdened heart that I put pen to paper, dear Diary, for today we have borne witness to a most bizarre and unsettling event that has shaken our community to its very core. As I made my way to the Church of St. Augustine this morning, I was met with a sight that I could scarcely put into words. The Church, once a bastion of hope and faith for our town, was nowhere to be seen. It was as if it had been plucked from the earth and whisked away by some otherworldly and unfathomable force.

I could scarcely believe my eyes, nor could the townspeople who gathered in the empty lot where the Church once stood. We stood in a daze, looking for signs of what had happened. The ground was undisturbed, as though the Church had never been there. The only thing that remained scattered on the ground was a miscellany of shoes and clothes, left behind by the visiting Jesuit monks. These devoted men had recently blessed our parish with their captivating hymns and sacred dances, touching our hearts and enriching the spiritual lives of our community.

While the day wore on, we searched the area for clues, but all we found was perplexity and sorrow. It was as if the Church had vanished into thin air, leaving behind only a deep sense of loss and bewilderment.

As the town's resident priest, I was called upon to comfort and guide the townspeople. I spent the day consoling the faithful, praying with them, and seeking solace in the Scriptures. We all prayed fervently for an explanation, but none was forthcoming.

As I retire to my humble dwelling, I am left with unease and uncertainty. What could have happened to our beloved Church and the dancing Jesuit monks who had visited us? Was this a divine intervention, a test of our faith, or some inexplicable and unnatural force? Whatever the answer may be, I pray that we may find it soon and that our community may once again find comfort and solace in the arms of the Church of St. Augustine.

EPILOGUE

As I sit here in my modest two-bedroom log cabin on the peaceful shores of Lake Anna in Virginia, retired and reflecting on a long and storied career with the FBI, the unresolved case of Laura Sommers continues to haunt me. Eight years have passed since that fateful summer, but the lingering mystery of her disappearance remains an enigma that I've been unable to shake, gnawing at the back of my mind.

Now, on this cold and blustery October evening in 2028, I've decided to write an epilogue for the collection of documents I've gathered about the case. These documents, some official and others obscure, span hundreds of pages and represent the culmination of years of investigative work. Despite many of these documents remaining classified, I have made it my mission to collect and preserve everything I could get my hands on.

The truth is, I harbor no illusions that this case will ever be solved. My superiors in Washington DC have closed the case and locked away the complete set of documents in the Central Records Complex, leaving only a classified version of the findings in the hands of the Chairman of the Ad Hoc Group of Paranormal Activities of the US Congress (Subcommittee on Space, Science, and Competitiveness). I highly doubt that any further progress will be made by this Group.

Much has changed since 2020, when the events described in this record occurred. First, the bright and talented field agent Thomas Bishop, who worked tirelessly on the case with a passion that inspired those around him, is no longer with us; God bless his soul. He tragically succumbed to incurable cancer at the Hospital of St. Mary, leaving a legacy of determination and commitment to the truth. The Indian cab driver, who steadfastly claimed (even under polygraph!) that he left Laura and her enigmatic companion at the entrance of a mysterious church building—a building that has never existed in municipal records—later married and moved with his wife back to Punjab, India, where he vanished without a trace, adding to the case's mystique. Laura's close friend Susan Donnay, once an invaluable source of information, unexpectedly recanted her testimony about the strange phone call from Laura, insisting that it never happened and that she fabricated the entire story. Her sudden reversal further deepened my suspicions about the case and the forces that may be at work behind the scenes.

Most intriguing, a 19th-century document discovered by John Levi, a reference librarian from the local archive, was dismissed by authorities in DC as "irrelevant, leading the investigation in the wrong direction." Consequently, it was never added to the case files. However, when I retired, I obtained permission to keep my own copies of these documents in my personal collection. As a result, I often find myself browsing through them, pondering their significance during lonely winter evenings as the wind howls outside and the fire crackles in the hearth behind me.

Tonight, as I recline in my inviting armchair, a cup of steaming Earl Grey tea in hand and enveloped by a cozy blanket, I find myself immersed in the pages of memos, transcripts, and reports yet again, seeking to decipher the perplexing mystery surrounding Laura Sommers' vanishing in the summer of 2020.

There are instances when I feel like I am on the cusp of a breakthrough when the seemingly unrelated fragments of the case momentarily unite into a coherent narrative that remains just out of reach. In those ephemeral moments, Father Damian's inscrutable diary entry, Laura's enigmatic phone call, and the Indian cab driver's baffling testimony appear to intersect, alluding to an astounding truth as it is unnerving.

But then, as swiftly as it came, the clarity dissipates, leaving me with a disordered heap of clues, each guiding me down distinct paths, each defying explanation. During these times, I am reminded of the sheer immensity of the unknown and the boundaries of human comprehension.

Thus, I persist in my solitary vigil on the tranquil shores of Lake Anna, my thoughts perpetually haunted by the elusive figure of Laura Sommers, her mysterious dance partner, and the secrets they carried with them into the darkness of the night.

Javier Garcia

October 13, 2028

Beaverdam, Lake Anna, VA

FROM THE PUBLISHER

As we were diligently preparing the manuscript for publication, working on copyediting, laying out the text, organizing the documents, and attending to the myriad tasks that a publisher typically undertakes, an unexpected event occurred that we felt compelled to share with our readers.

One morning, our office received a FedEx package with a return address that was, unfortunately, illegible. Curiosity piqued, we carefully opened the package to discover an unsigned letter addressed to our Editor-in-Chief. The letter bore the obscure title "Tango with God."

We cannot verify the origins or authenticity of this document, but after reading it, it might hold some relevance to the events detailed in this book. The letter touches on certain elements and themes that echo those found within the pages of our manuscript, and we could not shake the feeling that it was somehow connected to the unresolved mystery at the heart of the story.

Given the possible significance of this letter, we decided that it was important to include it as part of this book. It is our hope that by presenting "Tango with God" alongside the other materials collected in this volume, readers may find additional insights into the enigmatic case that continues to confound all those who delve into it.

We leave it to you, the reader, to draw your conclusions about the letter and its potential connection to the events described herein. And, in some small way, this intriguing addition to our book will bring us all one step closer to understanding the true nature of the mysteries that continue to elude us.

TANGO WITH GOD

"My name is Laura, and I find myself in a place where time and space lose their meaning. As my eyes adjust to the surroundings, I am transported into a world where I am intimately connected to everything around me. This connection opens the door to a new perspective, one where the lines between the individual and the environment dissolve.

The breathtaking beauty of this realm captivates me. Rich colors paint the landscape, while the fragrances of flowers and earth intermingle in the air. The gentle wind on my face and arms feels like a loving caress, and the music that permeates this world resonates deep within my soul, becoming an inseparable part of my being.

As I dance to the melodies, I experience a sense of liberation unlike any I have ever known. The rhythmical movements release me from the constraints of my past, filling me with happiness and inner peace that envelop me like a warm embrace. The world around me seems more vibrant and alive as if it is rejoicing in this newfound sense of freedom.

With each step, I soar higher into the sky, leaving behind the familiar ground. As I ascend, I feel an increasingly profound connection to everything around me. I am no longer just Laura; I am a part of this incredible world where the earth, air, water, and fire are woven into the fabric of my being. From the tiniest atom to the vast cosmos, I am intertwined with every aspect of existence.

The sun's gentle warmth and the whispers of the wind provide a comforting sense of belonging. The wind's harmonious tunes and the rustling leaves' gentle murmurs become my trusted companions, guiding me on a journey of self-discovery and unity with the world around me. In this newfound harmony, I am at peace with the universe.

Embracing nature and becoming one with it allows me to transcend the limitations of my human existence. In this state of pure connection, I can exist as part of the natural world, experiencing the wonders of creation without boundaries. My participation in this cosmic dance is a testament to the interconnectedness of all things, a celebration that defies the confines of time and space.

As my adventure draws to a close, I realize that it is not an ending but a new beginning. This experience has gifted me with a profound insight into my true home, a sanctuary in which I will reside eternally. The music and rhythms that have become such an integral part of me will continue to nourish my soul and guide me on my path, forever connecting me to the natural world and its wonders.

Thank you, David!"